0600179

D1503904

EJ
Parke
Parker, Neal Evan.

Captain Annabel /

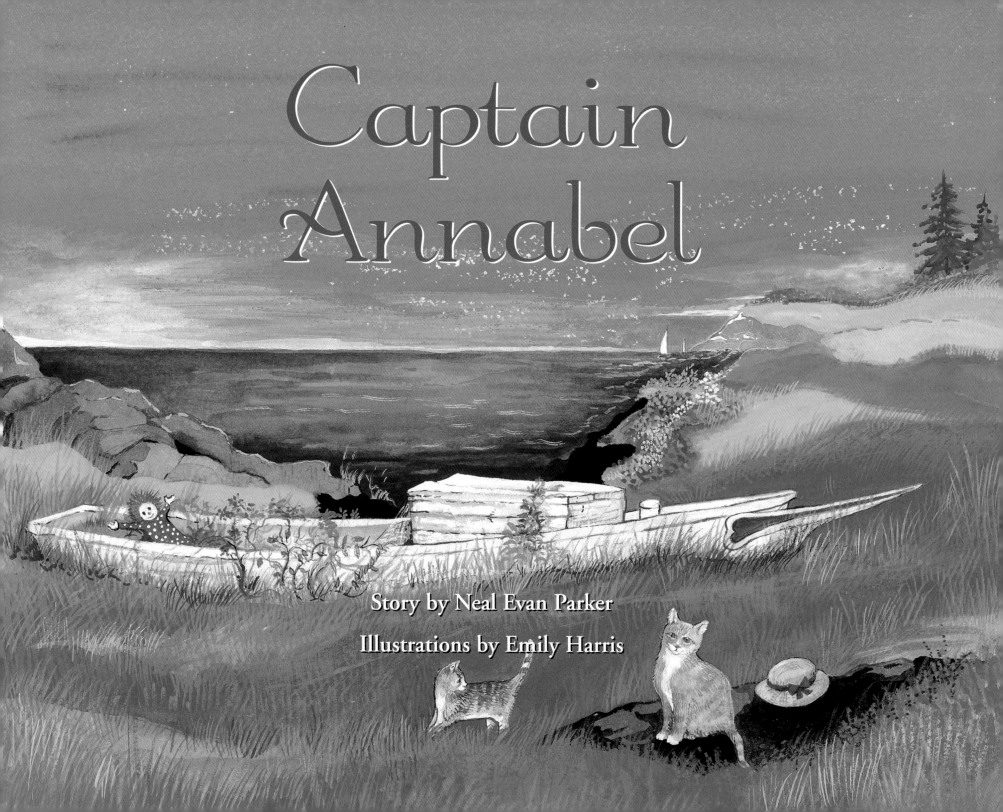

# Captain
# Annabel

Story by Neal Evan Parker

Illustrations by Emily Harris

Printed in China by Jade Productions

5  4  3  2  1

ISBN: 0-89272-653-9

Down East Books
Camden, Maine
Book orders: 1-800-685-7962
*www.downeastbooks.com*
A division of Down East Enterprise,
publishers of *Down East* magazine

Library of Congress Control Number: 2004109056

0 1021 0203430 7

## Dedication

From the author:     For my daughter, Annabel, follow your own path. I will always
love you.
And Emily Morand, former cook then mate of the *Wendameen*.
Any small person would be proud to grow up like you.

— Neal Evan Parker

From the illustrator:     To my sister Ann, who possesses a true artist's spirit, with love
and thanks.

— Emily Harris

Annabel's dad lived by the sea. He had an unusual planter in his yard.
It was actually an old sailboat that he hoped to fix up someday.

One summer, when Annabel was four years old, she climbed into the planter,
pulled out all the weeds, and yelled, "Boat!"

Annabel's dad was working nearby. He looked over and smiled. "Now two of
us think so, dear."

A moment later, as Annabel jumped and played in her boat, the sides of the tired, old craft gave out and fell flat on the lawn.

Annabel yelled, "Papa!" He knew what had to be done. They gathered up all the broken pieces and carried them into the barn.

All the rest of that summer, and for many summers to come, Annabel and her papa worked together fixing the little sailboat.

When launching day came, Annabel's dad said, "I have a surprise for you," and pulled away an old shirt that was hanging off the stern of the boat. There, in big, gold letters against the shiny, white hull was the name, *Annabel*.

Annabel, now seven, smiled shyly and said, "Oh, Papa." Together they pushed
the boat into the water, not even caring that their feet got wet. The little sloop
*Annabel* bobbed proudly.

Annabel and her dad spent as much time sailing together as they could. He taught her to sail and row, how to tell where the wind was coming from, and what the different colors of the water meant. They sailed together in good weather and bad. By the end of the summer, Annabel had become a good sailor.

Annabel's father let her take the boat out alone as long as she always wore her life jacket. She often saw her papa watching from the shore and she would take her hand off the tiller, wave, and yell, "Papa!"

Years went by. Annabel and her little sloop had many adventures.

One day her dad said, "I have taught you all I can. If you want to become an even better sailor you should learn from another captain."

Annabel was now eighteen years old and she took her father's advice to heart.

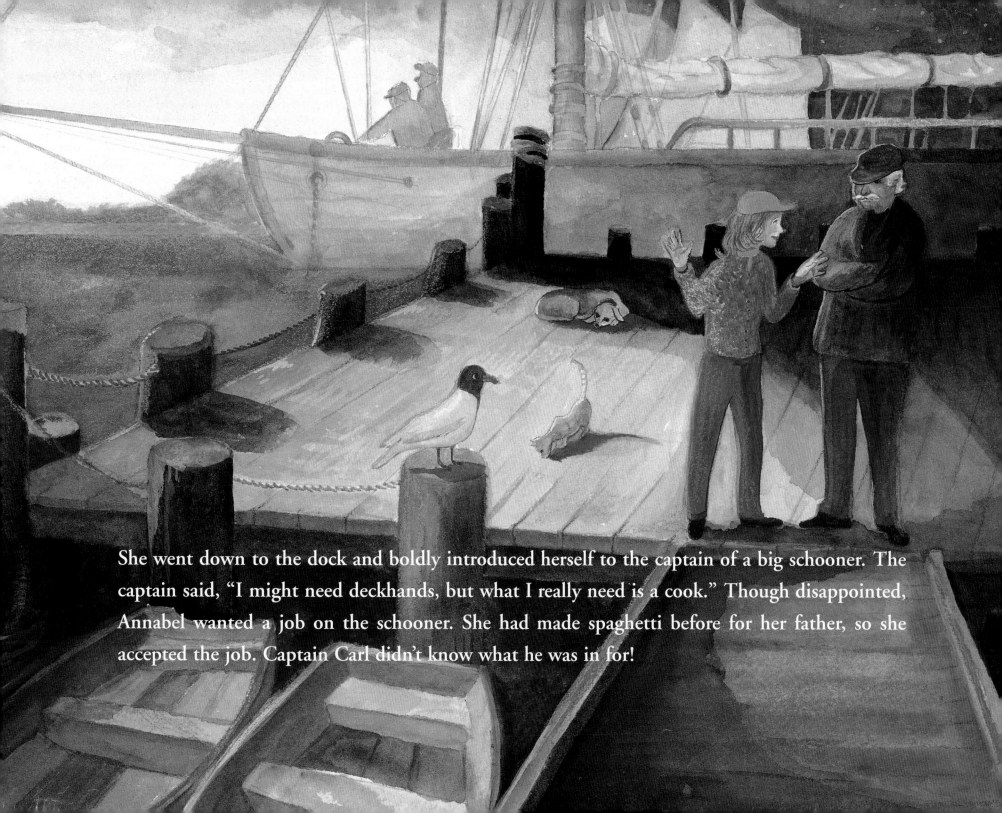

She went down to the dock and boldly introduced herself to the captain of a big schooner. The captain said, "I might need deckhands, but what I really need is a cook." Though disappointed, Annabel wanted a job on the schooner. She had made spaghetti before for her father, so she accepted the job. Captain Carl didn't know what he was in for!

It wasn't long before the crew and guests began to grumble about how terrible the food was. The bad food wasn't entirely by accident. While at sea, Annabel's thoughts were on sailing, not on cooking. Planning her next awful meal, she smiled to herself and said, "Not all girls can cook."

Up on deck the captain said to his crew, "This is the worst pea soup I have ever tasted. When we get to shore I'm going to fire that Annabel!"

Captain Carl had barely spoken when a big wind sprang up!

He called to the crew, "Drop the jib and ready the mainsail halyards!" But the crew became confused in the sudden storm and dropped the mainsail right on Captain Carl's head, knocking him out.

The wind blew the schooner so far over that Annabel barely made it up the ladder and onto the deck. As she came up the hatch, she saw instantly the danger the schooner was in. She grabbed the wheel and turned the vessel into the wind so that it would not knock the schooner down into the sea.

Then she ran to the bow and helped the crew take down the other sails. Captain Carl regained his feet in time to see Annabel save his schooner and those on board.

After the storm cleared and the excitement was over, Captain Carl turned to Annabel and said, "I am firing you. You are no longer the cook. Now, you are a deckhand."

Annabel learned everything Captain Carl taught her. Though she was a good sailor, the big schooner was a whole new world for her. Captain Carl was a good teacher and she learned quickly.

The next year Annabel was the first mate, second only in responsibility to the captain! At the end of that summer Captain Carl said to her, "You have done well and made me very proud. There are not many boats like mine around, and perhaps someday you'll be the captain of one. For now though, you need more experience at sea than I can give you." Annabel knew what the captain meant. They shook hands, hugged, and said goodbye.

Annabel found herself working as a deckhand on the New City ferry. It was her job to help people park their cars and to help tie up the ferryboat at the end of each trip. Annabel did her work without grumbling and impressed her shipmates. She soon learned how to steer and navigate the big ferry.

After a couple of years on the ferry, Annabel knew it was time to see new horizons. After all, a ferryboat only goes back and forth. She was now qualified to be a mate on a large seagoing ship! The new ship carried fuel up and down the coast.

Annabel worked hard and gained more and more experience with every voyage. But the part of the voyage she enjoyed most was when the big ship was entering and leaving port with the help of the powerful tugboats.

She loved the way they blew their whistles to signal each other and helped maneuver the big ship.

Annabel was all grown up now. She had sailed around the world a dozen times. Many was the long night at sea when she dreamt of her first little boat. She always wrote her papa long letters telling of the exotic places she had been. But inside she was always a little homesick.

Annabel loved the sea, but missed her home and family. She wondered how she could ever have both. Then, one day as the powerful tugboats were helping her ship into the dock, she knew what she would do next and it made her break into a big smile.

Annabel's father stood at the shore looking out to sea. He had not received a letter from his little girl in many months.

"She is very busy," he thought. "Or perhaps she has just forgotten."

He looked at the sea, half in a daydream, when he was suddenly startled by the sight of a handsome tugboat coming towards the shore. He heard its loud whistle.

Then, as the tug came closer, he saw his Annabel leaning out of the pilothouse window.

She was now Captain Annabel. Taking her hand from the wheel, she gave her dad a big wave. And as the tugboat came closer he saw in big gold letters against the gleaming hull the tugboat's name, *Papa*.

And Annabel could hardly
wait to tell her papa the tales
of all her travels around the
world.